The Cathedral

The Cathedral

A Parable

JEFF HOOD

RESOURCE *Publications* · Eugene, Oregon

THE CATHEDRAL
A Parable

Resource Publications
An Imprint of Wipf and Stock Publishers
199 W. 8th Ave., Suite 3
Eugene, OR 97401

www.wipfandstock.com

PAPERBACK ISBN: 978-1-5326-4089-6
HARDCOVER ISBN: 978-1-5326-4090-2
EBOOK ISBN: 978-1-5326-4091-9

Manufactured in the U.S.A.   NOVEMBER 27, 2017

Cover artwork: "The Source of the Queer" —Emily Jean Hood

For the Queens

Contents

The Drive

"If anyone will not welcome you or listen to your words, shake the dust off your feet as you leave that town."

—MATTHEW 10:14

The highway sun played tricks. What was I thinking? I guess I wasn't. Just when everyone gained some understanding in Jefferson, Mississippi, I had to up and go on a damn crusade. Riding in that car, I prayed for God to guide me. When I considered the guidance was leading me to Texas, I started to reconsider the whole praying business. Truthfully, seafood was all I believed in at the present moment. When I sat down at the only restaurant in all of Molasses, Louisiana, there was no way I could've predicted what was next.

The waitress approached the table and tipped her boobs at me while taking my drink order. While a little sidetracked, I managed to tell her that I would like a glass of sweet tea. Before leaving the table, she told me her name was Mary and asked, "What do you do?" I guess my satchel gave away that I was heading somewhere for something. "I'm a preacher," I replied. Mary blurted out, "God told me you were coming!!!" Mary raced over to the kitchen door. The first time I noticed that there was a bell on the wall was when she was ringing it. I hadn't noticed how many people were in the restaurant. Feeling something and climbing the counter, Mary declared at the top of her lungs, "We've got a preacher in the house tonight!" I couldn't believe my ears. Repeatedly, I resisted her gestures for me to come up. Then the entire restaurant started begging for a few words. I obliged. Letting out a fart that I prayed no one heard, I climbed up with Mary and started preaching. That short sermon was unforgettable.

> *"Jesus was an interesting guy wasn't he? The more I read about Jesus the more I question how I was raised. Honestly, I doubt our part of the country would've liked Jesus too much. While we're running around trying to keep gay marriage from happening, we forget that Jesus ran around in a skirt with a bunch of men. We shouldn't even need to have all these conversations about sexuality. The Bible is pretty clear that Jesus was gay. I guess all this gives new meaning to Jesus declaring his love for the world? In the light of such an interpretation, promiscuity doesn't seem so bad. Do you know what I mean?"*

I'd gotten so into the preaching that I hadn't done much looking around. When I finally did, I realized that someone was choking on a piece of fried shrimp on the other side of the restaurant. What I assumed to be the man's wife screamed, "Leroy! LeRoY! LEROY!!!" One of the cooks darted out of the kitchen and punched the old guy in the stomach. A piece of shrimp flew across the room and landed right on my shoe. The manager looked at me and yelled, "You almost killed Leroy with that crazy shit. Here, take these few pieces of bread and two fish. Don't be coming round here no more!" People have always told me that I don't have a proper understanding of place. Regardless, I shook the dust off of my feet and moved quickly toward the door. Before I completely got out the door, I yelled, "Y'all can all kiss the rainbow tattoo on my ass. I don't care what y'all say . . . that was a damn good sermon."

I ended up sleeping in my car that night. I guess I was too afraid of encountering more folks like the ones I did in Molasses. The yellow lights of the gas station were mesmerizing. I slept hard until someone banged on the door. A man with his erect penis pushed up against my window was standing there with a smile on his face. I rolled down the window slightly and asked, "May I help you?" "Are you Max?" "Nope, I'm Christian." "Oops . . . sorry to bother you . . . I was just looking for Max. This is a really popular spot for cruising and I saw your manicured fingernails and well I . . . I . . . You wouldn't want to fool around would you?" "No!!!" I cranked up the car and roared off. What in the hell had just happened? I'll never forget that night. Believe me . . . I've tried.

The miles quickened. Before I knew it . . . I saw the sign. "Everything's bigger in Texas." After one hell of a trip, I was finally here. Pulling over, I knelt down beside the sign to pray. I knew God called me to be a church planter and that's exactly what I intended to do. When a tough looking cowboy pulled over, I expected him to give me shit and tell me to leave. Instead, he asked to pray. After bowing my head, he said, "Repeat after me . . . Lord Jesus . . . I am a sinner . . . come into my life and forgive me of all my sins." Looking me straight in the eyes, he questioned, "Did you mean it?" I didn't know what to say . . . so, I just said, "Yes!" The cowboy goy all excited and started running around. When he stopped, he shouted . . . "Welcome to Texas . . . heaven." Before he left, he invited me to his Cowboy Church. Running to his pickup, he told me he had to get going . . . there were other souls to save. After he drove off, I realized something . . . everything smelled like shit.

I only stopped once. I had to. Everyone had always told me about Bullseye's. The joint didn't disappoint. With over fifty gas pumps and a convenience store as big as any grocery store . . . I was in heaven. As I put my mouth under the frozen drink machine and turned it on, I didn't count the cost. I called the property management company to let them know I was getting close. Before I arrived to the apartment, I started to feel it. Upon arrival, I ran to the toilet as fast as I could. I jumped onto the seat and took an incredibly loud shit. When I finished, I was so relieved. Tom from the management company greeted me in the living room. I overlooked him on the rush in. Due to the smell and theatrics of it all, Tom was in toxic shock. Before he finished giving me all of the instructions, he ran out the door. As he spewed his lunch all the way to his car, I shouted out, "I'm here to plant a new church!"

The First Days

"The first shall be last and the last first . . . "

—MATTHEW 20:16

Darkness filled those early morning hours. At the time, I loved it. I felt like I was the only one. Now, I know better. I moved quickly to press the coffee. Once the cup was poured, I took three deep breaths. I dared not take another. I felt like it would be wasteful. Every step reminded me of my loneliness. They say that you're never alone when you've got God. "They" are full of shit. The carpet crunched. I could feel the excess cleaner getting caught beneath my toenails. I thought about getting my slippers from the bathroom . . . but I knew the slippers were right next to the lotion and that would just lead to getting lost in yet another round of morning masturbation. I had to keep my mind right. God called me to plant a church not masturbate! Regardless of my will, I was stuck to the floor. Frozen in time, I could feel every bone in my body. I never thought I'd be alone. After I reigned in my thoughts, I retreated to the small balcony. I loved that place. I can still feel the cold Texas air. I opened the Bible and stumbled upon the feeding of the five thousand. I figured that if Jesus could feed the five thousand then that slut could certainly turn a miracle out of me.

For the first few days, I wandered around Jackson, Texas. I'd never been in a city so large or diverse. I met many different types of stories. The homeless man told me about the apocalypse. The teacher asked me to pray for her. The landscaper told me about the drought. The police officer demanded that I respect the Blue. The nurse told me about the healthcare shortage. I heard it all. I wanted more. There was a ravenous spiritual hunger growling within me. I knew I was doing the Lord's work. By the time Friday came around, I was more than ready for BoysTown.

I don't think anyone knew I fucked men back in Jefferson. Well, I guess the men I fucked knew but nobody else did. Mississippians are a flamboyant people. Nobody was suspicious of anything. I had the little rainbow flag . . . but that flag is so common these days. When I asked God to heal me, she laughed in my face. I quit asking and decided to live. That night, I prepared my body like I was preparing sacraments for the church. I guess in my mind . . . I was. I put on the nicest underwear I owned. I figured it would help me stand out in the crowd. When I got in the car, I turned on the ventilation system to keep from choking to death on my cologne. Nothing was going to stop me tonight.

When I got to the club, I used the valet service. Tossing my keys to the young attendant, I felt bad as shit. As the doors opened, I made sure I gently jiggled my ass back and forth all the way to the bar. An older queen I knew back in Jefferson taught me that trick. After ordering a drink, I told all who would listen that I was planting a church. No one seemed too impressed. One man leaned over and said, "We already have churches and we hate them all. Why do we need another?" One woman declared, "God is like shit. The best thing you can do is squeeze it out, flush and be done with it." When someone asked for my name, I proudly declared, "Christian." Three people laughed so hard they spit out their drinks. I guess they thought my life sounded like some crazy story or something. Everyone started bringing friends over to meet the guy named Christian who was planting a "Christian" church. Stiff drinks seem to make everything funnier. I got tired of being the blunt end of everyone's jokes. Humiliated, I knew it was time for me to go. Walking down the street to Balls, I was ready to get shitfaced.

Stumbling out a couple hours later, I ran into the hottest man I'd ever seen. I still don't know how much the alcohol factored in. When we started to flirt, I was in heaven. The celestial warmness extended to every crevice of my body. Before I got carried away, I had to make sure he was a Christian. I started preaching:

> "Jesus said, 'I am the light of the world.' In these few short seconds, you've brought much light into my life and I want to make sure that you know who the source of light is."

When I became assured he loved Jesus, I went in full thrust. As we started to passionately kiss, he stopped me and asked for some money before we went any further. Though I didn't even know his name, I would've given him anything he wanted. I was so in love. Before I could get one more kiss in, police swarmed in from everywhere. The female officer informed me that I was being arrested for solicitation of prostitution. My last words as I was being put in the squad car echoed throughout BoysTown, "But I came here to plant a church!!!"

With no friends or family close enough to get me out, I sat in that filthy Jackson County Jail for much longer than I anticipated. Throughout my time there, I met all kinds of people who were there for all kinds of crimes. I started building my church with those that Jesus referred to as "the least of these." I led meditations, yoga, lessons, readings and whatever else I thought would get people interested. When I finally stepped out of the cell to go home, I realized that

I'd been in that joint for 5 days. The guard told me that the charges were dropped for lack of evidence (aka they lost the tape). I was so happy that I shit slightly in my pants. "God is so good!!!" Over the last week, I'd passionately kissed the hottest guy I'd ever met, I collected a roster of over a hundred people for my new church and God busted down the jailhouse doors. "Hallelujah!!!" Walking out, I knew I was more than just a church planter . . . I was a prophet of God.

The Start

"I was in prison and . . . "

—MATTHEW 25:36

For over two weeks, I fasted and prayed. Jailhouse religion did a number on me. I kept rejecting the idea that I could plant a church with all these crazy ass people. I wrestled and wrestled. The list haunted me. While I knew God was calling me to plant a church, I was having trouble calling all the guys I met in jail. Then, it happened. The story of Jonah hit me like an oversized sack of potatoes. After sleeping with everyone he could get his hands on in Nineveh, Jonah ran away. God commanded him to go back and minister to the community. Just like me, Jonah didn't want to go back. When he finally did, the Ninevites were restored. Truth be known, I slept with too many men while I was in prison. I'd even enjoyed sex with three people at one time. I ain't proud of it . . . but that's what I did. Though I felt like I'd already done more than my fair share of pushing, I decided to heed the call of the queen of queens . . . my fellow sister . . . the Apostle Paul and "push toward what lies ahead."

The phone rang three times before I got an answer. "Tony?" "Yeah! Who's this?" "This is Christian from jail." "Oh shit! I didn't think you'd actually call." "I'm calling to invite you to the first service of our new church." "Will you and I get some alone time?" "Let's just keep it church Tony. The service will be at my home in two weeks. I know God is moving." "I do too. I can really feel it. I'm horny as hell." "Ok Tony, see you at church." Obviously, the first call went a little sideways on me.

Thinking that a public place would be safer for work, I met up with Roy at a coffee shop in BoysTown. Honestly . . . when I looked at the list of the guys that I was supposed to start my church with . . . I'd had sex with large number of them. Roy was a large guy with a sweet smile. I was really looking forward to reconnecting. When we saw each other, Roy ran up and kissed me right on the lips. Back in Jefferson, a public kiss on the lips between two men would've gotten someone killed. Relaxing, I reminded myself that Jackson was different. For over two hours, Roy and I enjoyed majestic conversation. In addition to committing to the church, Roy wanted to serve in leadership. I praised God. I knew we were ready to lead the church together. Before we got up, Roy asked me to put my hand on his thigh to pray for a blood clot he had. Though I thought I felt his penis, I just continued to pray, "Oh God we need you to push that blood on through!" Without provocation, Roy assured me that I hadn't touched his penis. I left invigorated.

Though I kept having all kinds of weird encounters, the church was taking shape. With about eighty people committed, we were ready for our first service. I wanted to meet with one last person before the night arrived. Charlie knew everyone. We met at a bar when I first moved to town and we immediately hit it off. In the course of conversation, Charlie made the drunken promise that he would bring over a hundred people to our first service. Though unsure of whether or not he could follow through, I decided to call him up. Charlie and I met at the same bar. I gave him all the details about our first church service. Looking about as serious as anyone I'd ever met, Charlie assured me that he never makes a promise that he can't keep. I began to weep uncontrollably and assured him that I would never forget his help. The hand came out of nowhere. Charlie slapped me clean across the face and shouted, "Pull it together! We've got a church to plant."

The Service

" . . . let each one of you serve his neighbor . . . "

—1 PETER 4:10

Have you ever woken up in total bliss? I did. The pillow felt softer than ever before. The sheets were the perfect temperature. The mattress floated under my body. The Holy Spirit filled every part of my body. I began to speak in tongues. I raised my hands to the sky. Electricity shot about the room. In the midst of it all, I could hear the voice of Jesus saying, "Plant that damn church!" Distracted by a hot wet tongue, I shot awake in bed. I knew it was Harvey . . . my new puppy. Had it all been a dream? I didn't have time to think about it. It was time.

Preparation looks different for every preacher. Today, I needed some deep prayerparation. For over an hour, I went to God for every person who might walk through my doors. I prayed so long that I think I even heard God say, "You've already named them twice." I guess even God gets worn out. Regardless, I stopped praying and started walking. Passing through the kitchen, I rebuked the donuts. On the way out, I looked in the mirror and saw Jesus.

Do you remember the wedding feast? I wanted our church service to look something like that. When the alcohol gave out, Jesus gave them more. I wanted Jesus to give us more and more and more. I wanted everyone to get so drunk that they even started dancing like Jesus. Can you imagine Jesus twerking his ass off? I bet nobody then or now has ever seen a robe bounce like that.

A short trip turned into a long one, I had to hurry. After I packed the supplies into the car, I raced home. Initially, I didn't notice the blue lights. While it is usually a good idea to stop for the police, I was tired of being targeted. I knew I wasn't going that fast. I was now.

Praying to God, I reached some of the fastest speeds I'd ever driven. The Holy Spirit was so thick in the car that I felt invincible. Then, it all ended. The squad cars peeled off and let me go. Driving away, I couldn't figure out what happened. When I got home, I turned on the television and saw that the biggest donut shop in town was on fire. God had intervened.

With just a few hours left, I rushed through the door. The smell was terrible. I looked around and saw a big pile of shit. Seconds later, I found Harvey hiding in the bathroom. I knew the connection. Regardless, I didn't have time to deal with it. Jumping in the shower, I washed off and tried not to masturbate. I didn't need any distractions. Jumping out, I dried off and went for the odor killer. The cologne smelled divine. Trying not to avoid gluttony, I held myself to six sprays.

Running back into the kitchen, I managed to get all the food and drinks out. As the time drew near, I grew nervous. Seconds felt like hours. Then, the doorbell chimed. Harvey barked loudly from his cage. I opened the door and it was my former pastor, Pastor Price. "I wanted to see what this bullshit church plant might be about and decided to bring some of my friends." Behind her, were four other dinosaurs. Together, they stomped in and sat down in the living room. I offered everyone food and drinks. While retrieving their requests, I heard a scream. Running back in, I realized that Pastor Price's friend Donald had sat in Harvey's shit.

I assured him that it was chocolate and gave him a pair of pants to wear for the rest of the night.

The doorbell chimed again, Tony and Roy came in together. Behind them, came a bunch more people. The doorbell rang incessantly. Before I knew it, I had over forty people. I couldn't even remember how I knew each person. I didn't care. When the musician arrived, we kicked it off with some funky shit. The only song I knew well was, "Lord, I lift your ass on high." Something magical was happening.

Right before the sermon, I heard a bang on the door. Apologizing, I went to see what was going on. True to his word, Charlie barged in with over a hundred people. "How did you get all these people here?" I figured it out quickly. Charlie placed a big block of marijuana on the table. Communion began early. Even Pastor Price and her friends took a few hits. It's probably an understatement to say that everyone was mesmerized by the sermon. I didn't disappoint:

> "Love is God and God is Love. When we make love we are making God. In the beginning was love, love was with God and love was God. Without love we are nothing. With love we are everything. For love so loved the world that love gave love's only begotten love that whosoever believes in love will not perish but have everlasting love. Make no mistake, love is everything."

One by one, people stood up and chanted over and over, "Love! Love! Love!" Everyone seemed so happy. I couldn't resist. I decided to give an invitation. "Who wants to accept the power of love tonight?" The whole room was ready. The Holy Spirit was strong in the place. Electricity popped around in the air. We sang and sang and sang. I think I even gave communion three times. People just kept wanting more. By the time the night was over, I'd collected everyone's information on clipboards and knew that I would need a much bigger space for our second meeting.

I got Donald's clothes out of the wash. Before I could apologize, he told me not to worry about it and that he'd even tasted a little bit of the exquisite chocolate he sat in. Looking around, every shred of food in the house was eaten and every drink was drunk. I even realized that someone had eaten half of a roll of paper towels. I gave everyone a hug and found myself alone with Charlie. "Do you want to make some of that love you were talking about? A victory fuck?" I was very tempted. Then, someone banged loudly at the door.

"Open up! It's the police." Charlie was gone before I even blinked. The last thing I heard him say was, "I'll take care of Harvey." I opened the door. "You're under arrest." Trying to run from the cops finally caught up with me. Though no one from the church remained, I yelled out, "I'll be back next week."

The Church

"... upon this rock I will build my church ...
and the gates of hell will not overcome it."

—MATTHEW 16:18

Before I knew it, I was out. To be honest, all of it seemed like a dream. I didn't have any money but somehow I made bail. Who saved me? I sat down on a bench and breathed the fresh air. In my ears, I heard a familiar voice. When I opened my eyes, there was no one there. I closed my eyes and listened, "Take the church to Swinging Dick's and I'll be there." I knew I was losing my mind. "Swinging Dick's?!? "I can't take the church to a gay bar!" Despite my hesitation, I couldn't shake the voice.

I started walking. When I got to the Washington Bridge, I paused to take in the sunset over the Jackson River. The world was on fire. The colors exploded across the horizon. Though I'd heard the voice before, it sounded different this time. "The colors of your church will be as brilliant as the sky." As tears streamed down my face, I raised my hands and closed my eyes. With each moment, I leaned further into the sunset. "Oh shit!" The next thing I knew, my feet were over my head and I was falling fast. The river raced toward me. I just knew that this was it. Right before I hit the water, I felt a hand grab my ankle. When I woke up in bed, Harvey was asleep at my feet. Next to my alarm clock, I found a note. "Keep your eyes open next time."

The apartment was a wreck. Each room looked like every cabinet and closet revolted. Unfortunately, I didn't have time to clean it up.

I had to call Swinging Dick's. The phone rang three times before Angela picked up. "Can I talk to you about renting the bar on Sunday mornings?" "You need to come over here right now if you want anything out of me!" I knew God wanted us to be at Swinging Dick's. So, I jumped in my car and raced over there. I passed one police car and prayed that I didn't get caught speeding again. I didn't need another incident. The rearview let me know that all was clear. Parking in the second spot, I ran upstairs. The back office was darker than I thought it should be. When Angela walked in, I knew why. For a general manager, Angela was nuts. Today, all she had on was a bra and a thong. "I'm going to need a fuck in order to close the deal." While I'd had a few relationships with women in my teenage years, I hadn't had sexual intimacy with one in a very long time. Regardless of my readiness, I knew that God would see me through. The church had to be at Swinging Richard's. When Angela dropped her thong, I was surprised that she was as hairy as I was. Regardless, I offered her my penis and we did it Pentecostal style . . . hands in the air, full body shakes and a whole host of tongues. The small piece of me that liked women was awoken with a vengeance. God made a way out of no way.

When all was finished, Angela leaned in and said, "Not only can you use the bar every Sunday . . . you can use it for free and I'm going to be a member of your church." Angela softly kissed me one more time and left. Though I know this was a strange way to secure a church location, I had to do what I had to do. With seating in the bar for over six hundred people, I figured we had much time to grow into the space. I decided to give our church a name that matched the ambition of our community . . . The Cathedral.

Over the next few days, I started calling as many people as I could. "We're meeting next Sunday morning at Swinging Dick's!!!" While most people were ecstatic, Bob didn't like anything abnormal. I think he came to the church to control it. I got line after line from Bob. "You're not safe!" "You're not really gay!" "Your lifestyle is anathema." "You're dangerous." "I can't believe there was marijuana at the first service!" "You don't have the right education to be doing this." "We can't meet in a bar!" I wondered whether Bob hated himself or me more. I tried to help him but he just wouldn't quit. On and on, Bob kept sending me crazy messages and slamming me on social media. This cat was bat shit crazy. Why does God afflict us with the calling to minister to everyone? Against my better judgment, I let it go. When he went silent for a period, I thought everything was going to be ok. Then, he pushed me to the limit.

The first morning as The Cathedral was amazing. Through a generous donation, our guitarist turned into a full band. People just kept on coming. We had donuts and coffee ready for every mouth and a seat for every ass. By the time everyone got settled, there were over two hundred people in attendance. We rocked out for Jesus. Charlie was on the front row winking at me. Pastor Price gave a stirring prayer about justice. Tony and Roy passionately held each other on the third row. The morning was perfect. When I arose to give the sermon, everyone cheered.

I was preaching hard on Jesus calling the disciples. Then, Bob started popping off. "You are a controlling, manipulative, psychopathic charlatan. I will not sit here and let you teach any longer." I'd had enough. I wasn't the only one. Everyone in the church started shouting him down. I realized I was going to have to have him removed. Larry and

David were our security team. When they approached Bob, he bit one of them. I demanded they not retaliate. Bob was drug out of the building screaming about what he was going to do to me. I reminded him that he would be arrested for trespassing if he ever came back to The Cathedral. Unfortunately, he did.

The Details

"The one who is faithful in little
will be faithful in much . . . "

—LUKE 16:10

The lights danced as the music pulled us deeper into worship. Hundreds and hundreds of people raised their hands and sang love songs to God. I did too. I still couldn't believe that God brought me to this moment. Never in my wildest dreams would I have thought that anything like this was possible. How was I leading the largest progressive church in Jackson? How? Occasionally, pastors need to stop and smell the roses. With a guest preacher filling in for me, I decided that today was my day. When Charlotte started to masterfully break down The Beatitudes, I checked out and let my mind wander a bit. The last few months at The Cathedral were not for the faint of heart or head.

Not long after we started meeting at Swinging Dick's, we hired a guitarist named Tim. He was the prettiest of pretty boys. Coming out of the Church of Christ, Tim was interested in experimentation. Often, this cat came to us straight from the bathhouse. As he ran in tardy, I didn't really know what was dripping off him. On some level, I didn't want to know. In the midst of it all, I tried to be as understanding as possible.

There was a time when I was interested in experimentation. That was before I got saved. Regardless, I'm sure you can imagine how all the folks at church took to Tim. That brother had boyfriend after boyfriend after boyfriend. The folks at our church were all over him. On multiple occasions, I pulled Tim aside and told him to tone it down. He didn't know how. By the time everything blew up, Tim was dating two men in the church and they were starting to get jealous. One was our video technician . . . West . . . and the other was our worship drummer . . . Steve. That Sunday morning, I was getting ready to preach when West projected a video on the screen of him giving oral sex to Tim. I guess this was intended to intimidate Steve once and for all. We got the video turned off and I managed to preach something. When it was all over, I went to Tim and said, "I'm sorry but you can't play in the band anymore." West left quickly. I haven't seen him since.

Oddly enough, our church grew when people heard we played a pornographic video in church. The Lord works in mysterious ways. Pretty boys don't make the best church musicians.

Amy was a runaway living on the streets of BoysTown. I met her late one night while out walking the streets trying to hear a word from God. When she called out to me, I almost didn't answer. I was in another world. However, I was trying to get better about being of earthly good. Stopping to talk, Amy told me her story. To be honest, there were details that I wish she'd left out. Nevertheless, I heard about the abuse, the drugs and the innumerable relationships. Touched, I invited Amy to live with me.

When Amy told me that she had a deep desire to be a minister, I made Amy the first intern at The Cathedral. Everything went well for a time, then some of Amy's old destructive habits resurfaced. Returning home early one night, I found Amy having sex with an underage teenager. Though every part of me resisted, I had to call the police.

Thinking back to my childhood, I wished someone had called to help me. Now, I minister to Amy in jail. We pray that she will only get probation when she goes to trial. Thankfully, Amy repented.

People don't know a damn thing about money. In those early months, we went through three treasurers. Suzanne was stuffing money into her bra. Luther was depositing money into his own account. Chris was putting money in his shoe. Money was going everywhere except to the church. Against my better judgment, we decided not to press charges against any of them. I tried to keep up with it for a time. How in the hell is someone with no background in accounting supposed to do all this shit? I decided to hire a permanent accountant. Money is always an important detail. Thankfully when I got the mechanics and processes right, we started rolling. Now, I love church money.

When I came back to the service and refocused on Charlotte, I began to realize that something was bothering her. She nervously repeated her lines over and over. Looking out into the audience, I realized that Bob was here with a gun on his hip. Earlier, I'd told her the story and asked her to be on the lookout. Though it is clearly posted that we don't allow guns, Bob was here to prove a point. I motioned for Charlotte to keep going.

When I confronted Bob and asked him to leave, he pulled his gun and pointed it at me. Pandemonium broke out. Then, Bob squeezed off two shots. I dropped to the floor. Pastor Price fell right next to me. Despite my pleas, Bob put the gun in his mouth and pulled the trigger. I will never forget the sight of his head exploding. Leaning back, I could see that Pastor Price was in trouble. "Hold on! This is not the end. Hold on! I love you." Looking up, Pastor Price managed to mutter, "I love you too." The bullet hit her heart and she bled out in my arms. I saw the life go out of her.

When the paramedics arrived, I realized that I'd been shot in the arm. I was so depressed. After much prayer, I decided to push forward. I knew that's what Pastor Price would've wanted.

The media swarmed me when I was released from the hospital. Everyone wanted to know one thing, "Are you going to keep The Cathedral open?" I shouted into the microphones as loud as I could, "HELL YEAH!" The following Sunday, half the city greeted us for worship.

The Explosion

"The day of the LORD is here . . . "

—Obadiah 1:15

In those days of grief and recovery, Harvey was all I had.
We went everywhere together. I never thought I could love
a dog so much. When it came time to return to church, I
couldn't leave him behind. In front of all the cameras, Harvey walked in.

Looking around, I couldn't believe it. People were everywhere. The building didn't have room to hold everyone.
The walls were covered. The bar was covered. The seats were
covered. The balcony was covered. The stage was covered.
Everything was covered. It was insane. People were chanting
repeatedly, "Ca-the-dral! Ca-the-dral! Ca-the-dral!" The
entire city came out to show their support. It was beautiful.

Right before the service started, the Fire Marshall informed us that the space was way beyond capacity. We had
to ask hundreds of people to step outside. Thankfully, we
were able to quickly erect screens to show what was going
on inside. When I came back in and walked to the front of
the church, I was reminded of Pastor Price's last wish.

There she sat stuffed on one of the front chairs. The
taxidermist did an incredible job of making her look so
alive. Earlier in the life of the church, Pastor Price told us
to stuff her and put her at the front of the church if she
died unexpectedly. I think she wanted us to have a visual

representation of her presence. I venerated her. When I was about to walk up the stage to deliver my first sermon since the shooting, I stopped to kneel and pray in front of her. As the cameras snapped and filmed away, I looked into her eyes with tears running out of mine. I felt like we'd resurrected her. The longer I looked at her, the more it looked as though she was going to speak. When her mouth started moving, I knew I was having a vision. Pastor Price declared, "Get on up there and preach. I'll be here when you get back." That's exactly what I did.

Looking out into the sea of people, my eyes locked onto one woman in particular. Bob's surviving widow Monica sat directly in front of the pulpit. A prominent Transgender activist in her own right, Monica desperately tried to get Bob mental help. Nothing seemed to work. After the shooting, she was one of the first people to call me. I felt so bad that she'd lost Bob. I knew how much she loved him. Stirred in my spirit, I couldn't let this moment past. I brought Monica on stage. In the presence of many, I wanted everyone to know that we forgave Bob and would stand by Monica. The entire room erupted. I knew God was working.

When I finally started the sermon, I firmly declared, "The Cathedral is a resurrection community!" Looking straight into the cameras, I shouted to thunderous applause, "We will not be undone by the terror of death!" Then, I hit the gas . . .

> *"We won't let tragedy make us hate. We love Bob. We're a resurrection people! We won't be intimidated by violence. We're too busy preaching peace. We're a resurrection people! We're going to be the strongest voice of peace and justice that this city has ever seen. We're a resurrection people! Hallelujah! We're a resurrection people! Hallelujah! Hallelujah!! We're a resurrection people!*

Hallelujah! Hallelujah!! Hallelujah!!! We're a res-urrection people!"

I collapsed in a hot sweat. Harvey licked me to make sure I was ok. The people wanted more. I didn't have more. Everyone in the room cheered wildly. One of the young women I'd been mentoring named Anne stood up and went to the microphone, "The power of God that you just felt is available at this church every week. The Cathedral is God's gift to Jackson. We thank you for your presence. Now, let's go be different in order to make difference!" I was amazed at her courage and tenacity. I knew that our congregation would be seeing more of her.

Multiple folks helped Harvey and I get past the cameras and into the car. I was exhausted. When I got situated, Charlie started to drive me home. "Stop!!!" I forgot something and needed to go back in. I couldn't leave her. By the time I told Charlie to go ahead, Pastor Price was buckled up next to me. After briefly dozing off, I woke up to find Harvey gnawing on her foot. Scolding him, I made Harvey promise to never touch Pastor Price again. When I got home, I put Professor Price in the guest bedroom and went to bed. Over the last few days, an explosion happened and it was more powerful than anything I ever imagined.

The Limelight

"Let your light shine . . . "
—MATTHEW 5:16

In the year after the shooting, my profile grew tremendously. Regardless of where I was, the people chanted, "Christian! Christian! Christian! Christian!" In city after city, I did interview after interview after interview. I was exhausted. After multiple failed relationships, I didn't trust anyone. Through it all, Harvey was the closest thing I had to a friend. Most of the people who helped me start the church got angry when they didn't get the accolades they thought they deserved. I was alone. After everything that happened, I learned to talk about God in superficial ways that didn't reveal the true questions that festered in my heart. I was struggling. I didn't know what to do. Masturbation seemed to comfort me more than anything. In spite of it all, our church was now huge. Literally, every gay man from within a hundred miles was there every time we opened the doors. After we hit four thousand people, I knew we needed our own space.

When I organized a committee, I did it just for show. I knew that I was going to be the one making all the building decisions. I found a piece of property right in the middle of BoysTown. Before consulting anyone, I bought it. Nobody seemed to care.

Then, I flew to San Francisco and found an infamous architect named ReRe to design it. Everyone was so excited. We didn't have to worry about money. People from all over the world were desperate to fund this unique project. At the groundbreaking, everyone chanted our name, "Ca-the-dral! Ca-the-dral! Ca-the-dral!"

We unveiled a statue of Pastor Price out front. We actually bronzed her this time. The entire facility was built within six months. The space was enormous. With room for over six thousand congregants, we were amongst the largest churches around. Before we moved in, we held one last meeting to determine what we would call the place. Almost immediately, someone blurted out the name we all knew we wanted, "The Cathedral!" When the day came to introduce everyone to our new space, I was particularly proud of three things. At the front of The Cathedral, we created a purple altar to memorialize our struggle. At the top of The Cathedral, we placed a phallic steeple shooting up to heaven with a cross coming out of the domed tip. Throughout The Cathedral, we made everything as ornate and glitzy as possible. I loved it. I could feel the Spirit of God in the place. When the day of our first service arrived, every major network broadcasted it live. Before I preached, I quickly masturbated in the bathroom. I guess I'd developed the habit to soothe my nerves. Moments later, I climbed into the raised marble pulpit and declared, "The Cathedral is here to stay!" Everyone clapped loudly. I basked in the beauty of it all. The cheering continued incessantly.

Though I poured my heart and soul into making the community as diverse as possible, The Cathedral grew whiter and gayer each year. I guess we should've anticipated the aging of our space. I wasn't thinking about the future. I was only thinking about growth. I guess I got caught up in the glow of it all. We sustained a regular attendance of well over five thousand people for all those years. I had the largest progressive church in the world. I wrote more books than I can count. Everyone sought my advice on everything. I was a renowned figure. For some reason, it wasn't enough. Over the years, I developed a habit of masturbating ten times a day just to keep my head on straight. When Harvey died on his twelfth birthday, I started to reevaluate things. For many years, I gave the church everything I had. I knew I couldn't give much more.

With ideas of quitting or retiring jumping around in my head, I knew I needed to find someone who could achieve wider diversity. I began to travel the country searching for someone to work with me for a few years and then step in as pastor of The Cathedral. I interviewed so many people that my head was spinning. I couldn't find anyone. While randomly visiting family, I met a woman by the name of Rev. Dr. Val Buffington. After a few minutes of conversation, I knew I'd found the one.

The Exit

"There is a time for everything . . . "

—ECCLESIASTES 3:1

We spent the afternoon packing. Mississippi can be enchanting. Glaring outside, I just wanted to go out and play in the leaves. I knew better. I had to get all of Rev. Dr. Val Buffington's final things into her small car. The rest was shipped a few weeks earlier. I loved getting to know Rev. Dr. Buffington's wife Letitia and her daughter Clarissa. The Buffington's were an amazing family. Upstairs, there was a purple box full of pictures that I took a second to look through. Lifting off the top, I got to see many intimate moments from her past. I knew this was holy ground. With each picture, we grew closer.

As we were packing up the final things, we talked about the future of The Cathedral. I loved every part of her plan. I hadn't been this excited about the church since we started. Rev. Dr. Buffington passionately kissed Letitia and Clarissa goodbye. Though she knew they would join her soon, two weeks was the most time they'd ever spent apart. Clarissa had to finish school. I'll never forget that final goodbye. We became the closest of friends on that car ride. We talked as if we were sprinting a marathon. We wanted to do it all now. Truth be told, we were still talking and not really paying attention when we passed into Louisiana.

The two trucks came from both sides. I saw the red one first. Rev. Dr. Buffington never had a chance. The truck dropped a log through her window. By the time we stopped, I was banged up to hell and Rev. Dr. Buffington's head was sitting in my lap. I thought these types of decapitations only happened in horror films. "What was going to happen to The Cathedral?" "What was going to happen to Letitia and Clarissa?" "What was going to happen to me?" The blue truck spilled gasoline. The car was burning. I could smell the flames on my flesh. I'd never felt such a sensation. The fire was rising higher and higher. The last person I saw was a huge trucker wearing a confederate flag hat with chewing tobacco drooling out of his mouth. He picked me up and saved my life. Before the car blew up, I heard someone assure me that things were going to be ok. Three weeks later, I woke up under the most intense white light I'd ever seen. I was covered in bandages. The doctor leaned over my face and said, "You're going to be ok."

Lying in that hospital bed for over six weeks was all I needed. I was done. Though it was nice to see news coverage all over television about my progress, I knew that I didn't have the passion to keep ministering. Phoning my leadership, I asked them to open up a national search for my replacement. Once the process started, I instructed my leadership that I would lead interviews with the three finalists. Is it bad that I already knew exactly who they would be? People stayed by my bedside throughout my recovery. There was one new person that I grew to love. Wearing his confederate flag hat that he had on when he saved me, Chuck refused to leave me alone. I grew to see him as a trusted friend. When it came time for me to go back to Texas, I told him he could go back with us if he left the confederate flag in Louisiana. Chuck obliged and became a trusted member of my inner circle. Though people were practically beating down my door, I refused to do any interviews. I honored the family of Rev. Dr. Buffington, preached like I'd never preached before and championed multiple local initiatives. All of it was well and good, but I just wanted to find the next pastor of The Cathedral.

Over two weeks, I met with the three finalists. Rev. Dr. Phillip Fuller was full of hot air. Everything he said was so dumb that I couldn't help but laugh. Rev. Dr. Fuller also kept farting in the interview. When your ass makes your potential employer throw up, you don't get the job. Rev. Dr. Bob Pinkston came in with a full on erection. I guess he thought he was going to fuck his way to the job. When I told him that I was calling the police, Rev. Dr. Pinkston got the hell out of there. After interacting with the first two sacks of shit, I was scared of what would come next. Then, Rev. Dr. Angela Utopia walked in. For years, Rev. Dr. Utopia ministered on the streets of Jackson. For some time, I admired her passionate work. She was a real prophet. By the end of the fourth question, I knew everything I needed to know. I hired Rev. Dr. Utopia right there on the spot. A black transgender woman of color was going to lead The Cathedral. The last thing I told her was, "It's time to shake it up baby!"

The Entrance

"Now I saw heaven opened, and behold . . . "

—REVELATION 19:11

Only my closest advisors knew about the hiring of Rev. Dr. Angela Utopia. Knowing that the congregation would be surprised, we didn't want anyone to find out early. I've always been a fan of big splashes. When I discussed my plan with her, Rev. Dr. Utopia assured me that she wanted the announcement to be as "shocking of a moment as divinely possible." Planning to roll her out in less than a week, we started working ferociously on the arrangements. On Friday, we sent out a press release letting everyone know that the next service at The Cathedral would be one of the most important ever. Not long after that, we sent out a similar message to the congregation.

I dined with Rev. Dr. Utopia the night before the service. Since neither one of us had a partner, we were able to take our time and get to know each other. Nothing was off limits. I told her everything I knew about The Cathedral.

Since I was the founder and sole leader for many years, everything I said was everything that needed to be said. When we got bored with church stuff, we moved on to more intimate topics. There were multiple moments that we just stopped and looked across the table into each other's eyes. I knew something was happening. I could feel it. This was too important of a moment to be distracted. I had to keep my mind on tomorrow. When the hour came, we were ready.

Sitting in my office, I thought about how my life was going to change over the next couple of years. I thought I was ready. Nevertheless, I had a job to do. When Rev. Dr. Utopia arrived, I encouraged her to identify as a transgender woman of color from the very beginning. Knowing my congregation, I thought it would be better to just make it plain. When we started to pray, Rev. Dr. Utopia ran her fingers across my Bible and rubbed my penis. I was beyond aroused. Things only got more heated when I reciprocated her advances. In that moment, Rev. Dr. Utopia's name changed forever. While I had enough sense not to continue, I realized I had strong feelings for Angela. Once I collected myself, the service was already going. We rushed down the steps. Angela and I waited to climb up on stage. In those fleeting moments, we confessed our feelings for each other. The loud music let us know that it was time for our grand entrance. As the cameras clicked and turned, we raised our hands together in triumph. The loudness and brightness kept me from being able to hear or see how the congregation was reacting. Then, it all abruptly stopped. I was alone at the microphone. Looking at all the people I'd shepherded for decades, I had no question how they felt or what was going to happen next.

> "For many years, I've struggled with how to transition out of my current role as pastor of The Cathedral. Rev. Dr. Val Buffington was intended to be my successor. Before I continue, I want to acknowledge that Dr. Buffington's family is with us today. The car accident changed everything. Lying in the hospital, I had much time to seek God about what to do next. I knew that we needed a national search. After looking everywhere, I know that we've found the best person. Rev. Dr. Angela

> Utopia has become an intimate friend of mine in
> a short amount of time. I'm impressed with her
> total package. Honestly, I've never seen someone
> who knows their way around a Bible like Rev.
> Dr. Utopia. I've never seen someone so passion-
> ate about the confluence of grace and justice in
> our world. I've never seen someone like her. I'm
> amazed. She's an unorthodox choice for an un-
> orthodox congregation at an unorthodox time. I
> ask all of you to get on your feet and welcome Rev.
> Dr. Utopia!"

I can always read their mood. I knew they weren't enthused
about our choice. I knew that many of them were racist. I
just didn't expect this many of them to be. Only about sixty
percent of the congregation stood to clap. Everyone else sat
in their chairs with their arms crossed and their bottom lip
puffed out. As Angela went to the microphone, we were in
trouble. There was a big part of me that didn't care. I knew
the time for change had come. Angela started her saluta-
tions and then the big reveal dropped.

> "I am proud to say . . . God has sent me to you
> today as a transgender woman of color."

Six of the oldest queens in the room fainted. The cameras
snapped away as one of the younger queens fanned an
older queen with a silk handkerchief. Gasps filled the room.
Multiple people walked out. Someone even had the nerve
to yell at me from the audience. I heard unbelievably of-
fensive words from what I thought were nice people. Before
it was all over, The Cathedral proved to be the most racist
and transphobic space I'd ever encountered. After the service, Angela and I had the best sex ever. We committed to
pushing through all adversity. For the next six months, we
fought was hard as we could. I'd always had suspicions our
efforts might be in vain.

The Escape

"The Lord will rescue me from every evil attack . . . "

—2 TIMOTHY 4:18

Day and night, we made love over and over. I couldn't get enough. I wanted to be wherever she was. We were so in love. Though I wanted to marry her, I knew I couldn't right now. Rev. Dr. Angela Utopia was the most amazing thing that ever happened to me. We kept it secret. I knew what the consequences were if anyone were to find out.

The Cathedral was in a tailspin. I tried to stay out of it. I wanted Angela to have the opportunity to prove that she could do it. While I tried to help behind the scenes, nothing seemed to work. The Cathedral became the epicenter of racism and transphobia. Maybe it always had been?

Throughout the period, I preached that a better way was possible. No one listened. Late one night, I told Angela that I thought our time at The Cathedral was quickly coming to an end. I don't think she believed me. I think she saw all of them for what they could be. I saw them for what they were. In the middle of her last sermon, we found out that it was worse than we ever imagined.

> *"Love God. Love your neighbor. That's the Gospel of Jesus Christ."*

Our services were broadcast live on local television. Whoever tuned in that Sunday, got much more than they bargained for. I don't know what it was about that line that set The Cathedral off, but things got wild quickly. I guess love has a way of revealing unbridled hate. I was sitting right behind Angela when it happened. In the middle of the sanctuary a man screamed, "Shut the fuck up you fake ass bitch!" Then, someone stood and yelled, "We don't want all that transgender bullshit around here!" From the other side of me, I heard, "Get that sack of shit off the stage!" Though I knew tensions were boiling, I had no idea this was even a possibility. I thought that building The Cathedral with white gay men would make it inevitably progressive. I was beyond wrong.

In the midst of the chaos, I froze. Before I could collect myself, I realized that a group of ten white men carried Angela out the door. The room turned into a mob. These folks literally ejected her from the church. "Where in the hell are the security guards?" I had no answers. Honestly, I was worried that the crowd that grabbed Angela was going to do something worse.

Unsure of what to do next, I oscillated between running after Angela or jumping on the microphone to try to calm everyone down. Deciding to split the difference, I grabbed one of the live mics and ran after Angela. When I finally reached her, I pulled the men off of her. I'd never seen such ravenousness. Angela looked up at me and said, "I'm ready to get out of here." I knew exactly what she meant. From the doorway of The Cathedral, I declared to the congregation, "Rev. Dr. Angela Utopia and I got engaged last night. I love her with all my heart. Due to your racism and transphobia, we will no longer be part of your lives. We are both resigning our positions at The Cathedral. Though I've loved you for many years, your actions today have given me reason to leave you with two words . . . fuck you." The congregation was shocked. We made our escape. Kissing passionately in the car, Angela and I drove off to make a new life. The road had never looked so promising.

The Vacation

"She makes me to lie down in green pastures;
She leads me beside the still waters.
She restores my soul . . . "

—PSALM 23:2–3

"You saved me." Angela whispered the words over and over again. I never got tired of hearing them. Not long after we arrived in Venezuela, we married on the whitest sand I'd ever seen. The local priest assured us that we were children of God. Those words are always nice to hear. We were the only three people at the ceremony. On the way down, I decided to take Angela's last name. In those seconds, I officially became "Christian Utopia." Once the pronouncement dropped, Angela and I ran and dove into the bluest water imaginable. Embracing in the consistent waves, I couldn't believe I was so lucky.

We bought a condo and started to make a life in the obscurity and absurdity of it all. Each day, I got better at training my brain to never think about The Cathedral again. Angela helped. We swam. We danced. We sang. We ran. We climbed. We did it all. Before we knew it, over nine months had passed. For the first time in both of our lives, we were happy. Then, things changed in an instant.

Walking down the street early one morning, someone approached me and questioned, "Christian Utopia?" Afraid to respond, I just froze. I guess I thought he would disappear. "I'm Quincy from The Cathedral and I was sent to make contact with you." For many weeks, Quincy followed me around. Honestly, I didn't want to have anything to do with him. I was done with all that bullshit. Each night, Angela encouraged me to at least listen to what he had to say. I wasn't interested. Eventually, I engaged him because Angela assured me that it was the right thing to do.

When we finally sat down, Quincy extended us an apology and asked us to come back to The Cathedral. Immediately, I said, "Fuck no!" Then, Angela said that forgiveness was the only way we could make a life worth living and that she was interested in returning as an act of grace. I started to have mixed emotions.

The Return

"The Lord will come like a thief in the night . . . "

— 1 THESSALONIANS 5:2

Perfect turned to partial in one plane ride. The ocean turned from blue to brown. The air went from refreshing to suffocating. The bounce in my step turned to a drag. What in the hell was happening? Everything was getting worse.

Thanks to Angela's reckless grace and compassion, I was being drug back to a world I tried to leave forever. The only thing that kept me from jumping out the window was Angela. In the midst of it all, Quincy warned me that there would be a greeting party from The Cathedral at the airport. I told him, "Unless you want to be embarrassed, you better phone ahead and tell them to go home." When we got off the plane, I couldn't believe all the media that was still interested in Angela and I. I thought a year would be enough to suffocate the frenzy. I was wrong. Until we got in the car, cameras and journalists confronted us at every turn. That shit was crazy.

Still confused, Angela and I spent three days at a retreat center praying about what to do next. When we felt a peace, I called the governing board of The Cathedral to tell them we were ready to talk. Over the last year, The Cathedral had declined by thousands, gained a nasty reputation and the physical premise was in ruins. There was no question in my mind . . . they were desperate. I guess you could call us their last chance. We were ushered into the secretive basement room where the board typically met.

I couldn't believe it was so cold. Noticing me shivering, one of the board members whispered that they were behind on the electric bill. For many hours, the board apologized repeatedly, outlined a plan to deracist and detransphobe the community, handed us a check for a hundred thousand dollars for what happened and begged us to consider coming back as their pastors. Before I said no, Angela loudly declared, "There is not a single chance in hell that we'll be coming back as your pastors. Try again."

After some discussions, we were both offered positions as "Dean of The Cathedral." We were to be figureheads. I didn't give a shit if they were offering me the title of "King of the Fucking Universe," I didn't want it. I just wanted to be done with it all. In the midst of my silence, Angela accepted the positions for both of us. Immediately, people swarmed us in jubilation. What had she done? I just wanted to be done with it. The entire situation felt very violent to me. On the way out, Angela looked at me and said, "How are you going to love your enemies from Venezuela? We're going to be right in the middle of them here." I felt betrayed. I was betrayed. Now, I was in a prison that I never chose.

The Dean

" . . . you will know the truth,
and the truth will set you free . . . "

—John 8:32

The months turned into a year. Despite the fact that I was personally miserable, my presence at The Cathedral brought the people and their money back. Nobody wanted to see what happened happen ever again, so everyone worked hard to fight against all prejudices. Hell, Angela became the most popular pastor at The Cathedral. As far as the leadership was concerned, all problems were solved.

They weren't for me. Angela and I were growing apart. While I didn't blame her, I quickly realized that she used me to get the gig she wanted. Now, Angela could stay at The Cathedral forever. Even though we went to counseling, nothing seemed to help. Though we weren't even sleeping in the same bed, I still loved her desperately. Part of our job was to assist The Cathedral in their search for a new pastor. After attending meeting after meeting and flying all over the world with the committee, we found our man.

Even though Rev. Dr. Charles Kingston was from Russia, our congregation thought that he was brought down from the Gods. With every step, Kingston showed off his physique. With every sermon, Kingston showed off his education. With every article of clothing, Kingston showed off his fashion prowess. Kingston had it all and then some.

We all knew that the community would love him. We were right. The congregation voted unanimously to call him as their pastor. I was there to congratulate him. I told him that his body was exactly what The Cathedral needed. Kingston loved that compliment more than any he received all day. Leaving the service, I told him I'd stop by his office to talk about our future work together. I wish I'd made an appointment.

When I walked up the steps, I was feeling better than ever. Kingston was doing a great job and I really liked him. Plus, he wasn't too hard on the eyes either. I was also getting to do the work that I'd always wanted to do.

Nevertheless, I opened the door and got the surprise of my life. Right there in front of me, I could see Kingston on top of Angela. I don't even know if there were any clothes in the entire room. Both tried to explain, but I'd already seen enough. I never had a second thought. I was done with it all.

I resigned my job as Dean. I divorced Angela. I dropped Utopia. I quit everything. I never talked to any of them again. I was back to where I started and it felt divine.

The Beginning

"In the beginning, God created . . . "

—Genesis 1:1

Mississippi remained as enchanting as ever. As the wheels turned, I knew I was heading in the right direction. Alone, I was exactly where I needed to be. For minutes and years and moments and hours, I had given my body and soul away piece by piece. Now, it was my time to utilize some of what I had left. Home called. There'd never been a progressive church in Jefferson.

Sometime later, I heard Angela won a sexual harassment suit against Rev. Dr. Kensington. Millions of dollars exchanged hands. I wasn't surprised. I knew we'd created a monster. Angela knew exactly what she was doing. I had to run away. I had no choice. I would've been next.

Though I tried not to think about it, I occasionally prayed that all the people that I left behind would finally realize how fucked up they were. As I grew older, I stopped praying for them. I was most interested in prayers that had a chance of working.

Upon the opening of the doors, my new church filled with loving and courageous women. Though I fervently resisted, they were adamant about the name, "The Real Cathedral." Time has been good to us. Daily, we strike fear into the heart of our backwards town. I love every minute of it. Looking back over the crazy years at The Cathedral, I realize the queerest thing I ever did was leave. I found God just outside of her walls.